D1351354

By whizzing broom and witchy hat.
By bubbling cauldron and magic cat.

By dusty spell book, old as time.
This book belongs to _Chelsea Buchan_ ,
Who whispers this spooky rhyme.

The BIG Wicked Witch Book

If you enjoy The Big Wicked Witch Book,
then you'll love these three huge collections
of fantastic stories:

The Big Book of Dragons

The Little Pet Dragon *by Philippa Gregory*
School for Dragons *by Ann Jungman*
The Bad-Tempered Dragon *by Joan Lennon*

The Big Haunted House Book

Bumps in the Night *by Frank Rodgers*
Spooky Movie *by Claire Ronan*
Scarem's House *by Malcolm Yorke*

The Big Magic Animal Book

The Marmalade Pony *by Linda Newbery*
Mr Wellington Boots *by Ann Ruffell*
The Wishing Horse *by Malcolm Yorke*

The Big Wicked Witch Book

The Cleaning Witch
CECILIA LENAGH

Broomstick Services
ANN JUNGMAN

Fisherwitch
SUSAN GATES

Hippo

Scholastic Children's Books,
Commonwealth House, 1–19 New Oxford Street,
London, WC1A 1NU, UK
a division of Scholastic Ltd
London ~ New York ~ Toronto ~ Sydney ~ Auckland

Published in this edition by Scholastic Ltd, 1998

The Cleaning Witch
First published in the UK by Scholastic Ltd, 1997
Text copyright © Cecilia Lenagh, 1997
Illustrations copyright © Serena Feneziani, 1997

Broomstick Services
First published in the UK by Scholastic Ltd, 1990
Text copyright © Ann Jungman, 1990
Illustrations copyright © Jan Lewis, 1995

Fisherwitch
First published in the UK by Scholastic Ltd, 1998
Text copyright © Susan Gates, 1998
Illustrations copyright © Rhian Nest James, 1998

Cover illustration copyright © Anni Axworthy, 1998

ISBN 0 590 54357 1

Typeset by M Rules
Printed by WSOY, Finland

2 4 6 8 10 9 7 5 3 1

The rights of the authors and illustrators to be identified
respectively as author and illustrator of their work have
been asserted by them in accordance with the
Copyright, Designs and Patents Act, 1988.

Contents

The Cleaning Witch

CECILIA LENAGH

Illustrated by Serena Feneziani

To my parents –
a small return for their gift
of a childhood full of books.
C.L.

Chapter 1

Grizelda Grimthorpe was grumpy. Business just wasn't what it used to be.

"Nobody wants a witch these days," she muttered, rubbing furiously at her crystal ball with a duster. "I wish I had another job, indeed I do!"

As she spoke, the crystal ball glowed. Within it appeared the "Situations

Vacant" column from the *Grindley Echo*. Picked out in red was the small advertisement,

"Cleaner wanted. Apply Miss Addle's Academy for Artistic Children."

"Hmm! Speak when you're spoken to!" said Grizelda, throwing her duster over the crystal ball.

She stomped outside, looked for a moment at her sign –

WHICH WITCH LTD.
HORRORSCOPES CAST. PRINCES
PUNISHED. SLEEPING SPELLS
GUARANTEED FOR A HUNDRED YEARS.
APPLY WITHIN.

– and sighed. "Must *be* about a hundred years since I frogged anyone," she said. "But, though I say so myself, when I frogged 'em, they *stayed* frogged!"

Ten minutes later Grizelda locked the front door of her cottage with a huge key, straightened her best hat – the one with the wax cherries and the stuffed bird – placed her black bag in the front basket of her rattly old bicycle and set off for town.

As she puffed up the steps to Miss Addle's Academy for Artistic Children, Grizelda could see, even from the outside, that a cleaner was badly needed. The

windows were grimy inside and out, and the paintwork around them more grey than white. Grizelda shook her head and tut-tutted at the discoloured brass doorknob and knocker on the big double front doors. She couldn't walk past without giving the letter-box a quick rub with her hanky.

Inside, however, she could see that some efforts had been made to make the school bright and cheerful. Home-made display boards (only *slightly* lopsided) lined the walls of the big airy entrance hall, and proudly displayed the colourful paintings and collages of the younger pupils. Shiny mobiles danced in the air, while papier-mâché sculptures and wooden carvings stood here and there. Near the foot of a broad staircase, a red-haired girl and a tall boy were moving another sculpture into place. They were laughing and chattering as they struggled with a lumpy, frog-like object, which reminded Grizelda of a bad dream she'd had once after a late supper of toasted cheese.

Grizelda coughed loudly, and the boy turned round. "Oh, sorry, we were so busy we didn't notice you there! Er . . . did you

want to see Miss Addle? I'm afraid she's a bit . . . um . . . tied up just now." The children grinned at each other. "She's had to step in as a model for the seniors' drawing class, 'cos we can't afford to pay for a real artist's model this term, she says. My name's Ben and she's Sarah. Can we help?"

"Looks like *you're* the ones who could use some help around here," sniffed Grizelda, looking about her. "I don't know as I've ever seen so much dust in one place before."

"Yeah, that's what my mum says," agreed Sarah. "She says it's a disgrace and bad for my asthma, but my dad says it's not Miss Addle's fault that cleaners won't work for what she can pay them. He says my mum wouldn't work for it either."

"Does he, indeed!" said Grizelda thoughtfully, but before she could enquire further a tall, thin figure wrapped in trailing draperies appeared at the head of the stairs. It glided down the stairs, stretching out a hand towards Grizelda. For one moment Grizelda wondered whether the Academy had its own artistic ghost, but Sarah and Ben ran forward and

as the "ghost" reached the bottom step
they began to unwind it. What finally
emerged was a pleasant, harassed-looking
woman, dressed in an ordinary skirt and
jumper.

"Thank you, children," she said, mopping her pink face with a piece of her discarded wrappings. "My, it was hot in there! I do wish the seniors had chosen something else for their drawing project! If I'd realized I had to be 'a mysterious veiled figure' this week I'd have worn a cotton frock today, or even my bathing suit!" She bundled up the material and handed it to Ben and Sarah. "Put these into the dressing-up box, please, on your way back to class. Isn't it almost time for your gym lesson? You'd better hurry, and don't forget to change your shoes!"

Sarah and Ben, arms full, hurried off. Miss Addle turned to Grizelda. "Good afternoon," she said warmly, still sounding rather flustered. "I am Miss Addle, the Headmistress of the Academy. Have you come to enrol a new pupil,

Mrs . . . er. . .?" Her eyes brightened
hopefully as she tugged at her rumpled skirt
and hastily smoothed her faded, brown
hair.

"The advertisement
said 'Cleaner
wanted'," said
Grizelda firmly. "It
didn't say anything
about *pupils*. If it was
pupils you wanted,
you should have said
so. My name is
Grizelda Grimthorpe,
and I've come about
the cleaning." And
not a moment too
soon, by the looks of
things, she added to
herself.

Miss Addle eyed Grizelda. A cleaner? Was she *quite* suitable? Really, with her short, dumpy figure, all that fly-away grey hair escaping from its untidy pony-tail and those bright green eyes, Mrs Grimthorpe looked – well, almost like a witch!

"I do need someone right away, Mrs Grimthorpe," she said doubtfully, "but I'm not sure . . . and really, you see, I can't pay much . . . so perhaps. . ."

As she spoke the phone rang in an office nearby. Miss Addle hurried in to answer it, leaving the door open behind her. While she waited for Miss Addle to return, Grizelda took a good look around. Once upon a time the Academy had been a grand house, with fine furniture and glittering chandeliers. Now the unswept halls and grimy stairways echoed to the running feet and happy voices of paint-smeared children, as a bell rang and classes surged from one room to another. Sunlight streamed in through a skylight window, and dust turned and danced in the shaft of golden light.

Through the open door of the Headmistress's office, Grizelda could see Miss Addle standing at her desk. She didn't seem to be enjoying her phone call. Her pink face had turned pale, and two little frown lines cut deep into her forehead. Suddenly she gasped and her quiet voice rose in protest. "Close the school? But, Mr Blockett, you can't do that!" A voice on the other end of the phone could be heard faintly, like a faraway duck quacking.

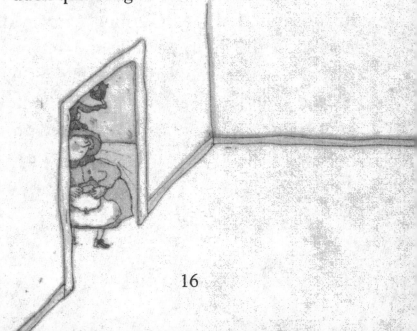

"Yes, I *know* it's a bit run-down at the moment, Mr Blockett, but we don't make much money and cleaners cost such a lot these days. But to say we should close the school . . . the children *love* it here . . . we can't just turn them away!"

"Quack! Quack!" went the phone for a long time while poor Miss Addle looked more and more unhappy.

Grizelda frowned. Suddenly, she decided that she liked the look of the school. It *was* dirty and messy, but that could be fixed. The school had a happy, friendly, lively atmosphere. Those two youngsters, Sarah and Ben, had actually looked pleased to see her. That was such a pleasant change from her lonely cottage. There, she had no one to talk to but her cat and that uppity crystal ball, and she had already spring-cleaned the cottage twice over until it shone. Close the school? Just when Grizelda had found herself the right job? No – not if *she* had anything to do with it!

Grizelda Grimthorpe fixed her bright green eyes on Miss Addle, twiddled her fingers – two bright purple sparks flew into the air – and muttered,

"Dirt and dust must now obey;
Grizelda Grimthorpe's come to stay!"

Miss Addle put down the phone, rubbed her forehead wearily and looked at Grizelda. "Yes, Mrs Grimthorpe, you'll do splendidly," she heard herself saying, though she felt sure she had really meant to say quite the opposite. "Can you start this afternoon? I'll show you where everything is kept – mops and brushes and so on."

"I'll use me own broom, if you don't mind," said Grizelda firmly. "It's used to me, like – it knows me ways. I don't want to go breaking in new brooms at my age."

Miss Addle blinked, hesitated for a moment, then she smiled. What difference could a broom make, after all?

"Do whatever you think is best, Mrs Grimthorpe," she said.

Chapter 2

Grizelda returned to the school later that day, just as the last few pupils straggled out through the big gates on their way home. Ben gave her a cheery smile and a thumbs-up sign as he passed.

A long, shiny, black car sat outside the front door. It looked important and official. Miss Addle came out of the school, nervous and flustered, with a man in a dark suit. He was frowning and shaking his head.

"If there isn't a big improvement, Miss Addle, I'm afraid we'll have no choice.

Can't have the pupils working in all this dust and dirt, can we? Parents are starting to complain! Doesn't look good! This building and the grounds would fetch a lot of money, you know. As trustees, we have to do our best. . ."

"But, Mr Blockett. . ." pleaded Miss Addle as he got into the back seat of the car.

He banged the door shut and wound down the window. "Remember, a big improvement, Miss Addle! I'll be keeping a close eye on things from now on!"

Grizelda watched the car sweep away, her green eyes hooded. Somebody's manners could do with a big improvement, she thought. Somebody needed to be taught a lesson! Grizelda set to work to do just that. She rolled up her sleeves, patted her broom and followed Miss Addle indoors.

Miss Addle looked pale and worn. "I think I'll go home and rest," she quavered. "It's been a very difficult day. Just do whatever you think is best, Mrs Grimthorpe. I'm afraid your job may not last for long, if Mr Blockett has his way. Oh, dear, if *only* we could prove that the school is worth saving!"

She gazed around the dusty hall, and absent-mindedly patted the nose of a lumpy black and white papier-mâché cow. "We used to win first prize in all the inter-schools art competitions, you know," she said. "Parents used to be proud to send their children here . . . but somehow, all our materials have become so expensive. We don't charge high fees, you see, and it gets harder and harder to manage. Most of the parents couldn't pay higher fees even if we asked them to. Some of them can only just about manage as it is, and I won't ask them to pay more than they can afford."

With a last sad look around, Miss Addle went to fetch her coat, leaving Grizelda to her first evening's work.

Grizelda began cleaning the first classroom. Paper leaned against the walls in unsteady piles or stood in dusty rolls stacked in corners. Giant, economy-sized tins of glue dribbled stickily on to shelves and down to the floor. Tubes of paint, minus their tops, mingled their contents in sludgy brown puddles in the sink. In one corner stood a large clay-spattered bin, its lid half off. In another was a table, holding a cage labelled "Jeremiah". Something inside moved, and scuttered under a heap of wood shavings.

Grizelda looked closer. A long, pink, ribbed tail poked out of the shavings. She tickled it with a paintbrush. There was a small explosion among the shavings and a white rat appeared. A small, ordinary-looking rat with beady pink eyes. It sat up on its back legs and twitched its nose.

"Well," said Grizelda, "you're a sorry-looking specimen and no mistake!" The rat began washing its face, peering at her warily between swipes of its paws. "Hmm, 'spect you're as dusty as the rest of the place!"

Miss Addle's footsteps clicked past the classroom. She called goodbye. The front door shut with a bang which raised small clouds of dust and made the cage shake. The rat jumped nervously and disappeared under the wood shavings. Grizelda laughed and went back to work. She swept her broom – one of the old-fashioned, twiggy kind – through the dust, with a swishing sound which whispered through the empty classroom.

Chapter 3

Slowly, Grizelda Grimthorpe began to feel almost lonesome, all by herself in the echoing building. She wished there was someone to talk to while she worked. She glanced at the rat Jeremiah, which now peered from its cage with inquisitive eyes.

"Wish *you* could talk!" she said. She

29

gave it a long, considering look, then,
"Don't see why not," she said suddenly.
She twiddled her fingers – purple sparks
sizzled and spluttered like fireworks – and
muttered,

"By my bird and cherry hat,
What I need's a talking rat!"

The rat quivered, its outline shaking like something seen through a purple heat haze. Then it settled, solidified, and there sat a much larger white rat, sleek and fat, with purple eyes. It began to groom its silky coat from nose to tail, then, satisfied with its appearance, it made a low bow to Grizelda.

"Hmm," sniffed Grizelda, "handsome is as handsome does, my old mother used say, but at least your manners are better than *some* as I could mention. You'd better come out of there, for a start. I can't abide to see animals in cages."

"I quite agree, madam," said the rat in an unexpectedly sweet, high voice, "and I am indebted to you." As the cage door squeaked open he hopped out and surveyed the classroom, nose twitching, whiskers aquiver with excitement. "Such a lot to explore!"

"That's an idea, right enough," said Grizelda Grimthorpe. "I'll join you."

Clicking her fingers at the broom Grizelda muttered,

"Make the dust fly, besom broom,
Clean this higgledy-piggledy room!"

A swirl of lavender sparks settled over the broom where it stood propped against an easel. Jerkily, the broom rose and began to sweep briskly. "And mind you sweep *under* the desks too!" Grizelda reminded it firmly.

Behind her the lid fell off the clay-spattered bin. Jeremiah the rat balanced precariously on the edge of the bin, peering in. Inside, bundles wrapped in wet cloths gave off the strong, cold smell of damp clay. The rat sneezed.

"Clay!" said Grizelda happily. "I haven't made a good homunculus in a long time. I used to make 'em all the time when I was at school meself."

"Ah!" said the rat politely. "You were an artistic child, madam?"

Grizelda chuckled. "When I was a young apprentice witch, and *that's* many a year ago, making a few dozen little clay mannikins and bringing them to life was our usual punishment for being naughty – like writing a hundred lines would be nowadays."

"Ah!" said the rat, even more politely. "Artistic and spirited, madam – artistic and spirited! A happy combination, I'm sure."

Grizelda watched the broom working away in the dusty corners. "What I need here," she murmured thoughtfully, "is a few extra pairs of hands, and I think I know where to get them."

She pulled out a heavy wodge of damp clay and thumped it down on a table. "*If* I haven't forgotten how. . ." she said, and unwrapped the bundle.

Chapter 4

Jeremiah watched with interest. Grizelda's fingers flew – pinching, prodding, tweaking the solid mass of clay. Purple, violet and lilac sparks sputtered and sizzled around her hands, hissing where they landed on the cold clay. The witch's lips moved silently, like someone reading an unseen story. Soon, the table held an array of stubby clay figures, each about twenty centimetres high, roughly fashioned but all individual. Their faces had round, hollow eyes (made by a pencil end) and blobby button noses. Grizelda stepped back, head on one side and lips pursed.

"Not my *best* effort," she said critically, "but it will have to do. Now, let's see . . . how did the rest of the spell go. . ."

Jeremiah raised a paw. "How about –
'Little workers made of clay,
Never need a holiday'?"

"I can see you're going to come in handy!" Grizelda said with a laugh, repeating the rat's rhyme as she waved her hands in an odd motion over the collection of stumpy clay figures.

Jeremiah's eyes brightened. Each little figure briefly gave off a bright purple glow. As they changed colour their sticky clay appearance changed too. There was a sudden strong smell of lilac. (Jeremiah sneezed again.) The dumpy figures stirred, slowly turning their heads and stretching their fat little arms and legs, as if to check that they really worked. Chattering softly, they admired their own and each other's pink and purple colours. Then they all turned to Grizelda and waited, looking as expectant as their round faces allowed.

"Now then," said Grizelda briskly, "there's a lot to be done. . ."

As she marshalled her troops for The Great Clean-Up, no one noticed the faint crunch of gravel as a bicycle wobbled to a halt at the back door.

Mr Blockett climbed carefully off his bicycle and looked around. If anyone had been there to see him, they might have wondered at the change in his appearance.

Gone was the smart dark suit and the polished shoes. In their place Mr Blockett wore ordinary jeans, an old sweatshirt and a pair of trainers. He no longer looked like a smart, respectable businessman. The only odd note was the clipboard he took out of his bicycle bag. Quietly he opened the back door and disappeared inside the school.

Meanwhile, Grizelda had organized the clay people – whom she called "claggies" – into a cleaning brigade. Swinging on curtains to shake out the dust, sliding down banisters on toboggans made of dusters, venturing bravely under low cupboards in search of all the pencil ends, beads and fluff which make their homes in such spots, the claggies were an invincible army of dust-busters.

Grizelda's old broom, which jealously

creaked and groaned in an alarming fashion when the claggies ventured too close, continued to swirl around the floor. Jeremiah joined in the spirit of the occasion and went from desk to desk, polishing off anything edible he could find – biscuit crumbs, furry old toffees and the like.

Grizelda floated herself up to the big chandelier in the hall, and became absorbed in washing and wiping every crystal dewdrop until it sparkled. She

hummed loudly
and a little off-key
as she dripped
water on to
anyone unwise
enough to linger
underneath.

Nobody noticed Mr Blockett. He poked and pried in the kitchen, making notes on his clipboard for the urgent report he planned to make to the Board of Trustees, recommending the immediate closure and sale of the school. He knew just who

45

would like to buy such a valuable property, and there would be a fat reward in it for him if he could get old Milligrew, the Chairman, to agree that the school was too run-down and unsuccessful to continue.

Mr Blockett silently crept out of the old-fashioned kitchen, which to his disappointment had been kept clean and tidy. Time to look upstairs; he sneaked up the back stairs to the first floor. As he tiptoed along the corridor towards the main landing and the front staircase, he paused – what *was* that strange, droning sound, and those odd, soft, chattering noises?

Chapter 5

Mr Blockett proceeded cautiously. It would be embarrassing to have to explain his presence, if someone found him now. The crooning grew louder. He came to a turn in the corridor and peeped around the corner. To his astonishment, he saw a stout, grey-haired old woman slowly floating down through the air from a large sparkling crystal chandelier which hung over the stairwell just ahead of him! Water dripped from a cloth in one hand while her other hand steadied a floating yellow plastic bucket.

"I must be seeing things," moaned Mr Blockett. "It's all this overtime!" As though drawn by an irresistible force he crept out and looked over the banister, down into the front entrance hall, where the strange old woman had just landed.

"Jeremiah!" she shouted.

From the nearest classroom a large white rat bustled out, wiping its mouth. It bowed politely and said in clear, fluting tones, "You called, madam?"

Mr Blockett raised a trembling hand to his forehead and sank to his knees. He closed his eyes and began to count to ten silently. Four. . . Five. . . All a dream! . . .

Six. . . Seven. . . Just overwork! . . . Eight. . . Nine . . . something cold brushed against his hand. He opened his eyes and found himself staring into two round, hollow eyes in a fat little purple face.

Mr Blockett let out a strangled yell –
which seriously alarmed the poor claggy –
fell straight over backwards with a crash,
got to his feet and ran!

Darkness had fallen before Grizelda
Grimthorpe felt satisfied with the changed
appearance of Miss Addle's Academy.
Floors gleamed; shelves were models of
ordered neatness, with papers, paints and
other bits and pieces all stored away in
labelled containers.

Finally the claggies assembled, chattering and squeaking softly, back by the clay bin (now minus its splatters of old, dried clay). Jeremiah, who had grown quite attached to them all, looked anxiously at Grizelda.

"What now, madam?" he asked quietly.

"Time to undo my spells," said Grizelda.

"Everything, madam?" said Jeremiah sadly. He had so enjoyed his new powers and appearance.

Grizelda hesitated. "I must turn the claggies back to clay," she said slowly. "They won't last past midnight anyway, and if I leave them, it'll only spoil the clay they're made of, letting it dry out. That was a powerful spell I put on it, and it may leave some magic in the clay, but that won't do any harm. No one will notice. Waste not, want not! But you, now . . . that's another matter."

Jeremiah looked hopeful.

With sudden decision, Grizelda declared, "I know! If no one but me can see the changes in you, or hear you speak, then what they don't know won't hurt 'em, will it? And I have a feeling you're going to come in very handy here! I'll need someone who can keep an eye on things for me during the day, and give me a bit of a hand – I mean, a bit of a paw – at night."

With a twiddle of fingers and a shower of
sparks, Grizelda muttered,
"Back to clay let claggies go,
But Jeremiah none shall know.
By my bird and cherry hat,
None shall hear a talking rat!"
Where the claggies had stood, there was
now a heap of clay, to which a faint smell
of lilac still clung. Ignoring Jeremiah's
wistful sigh, Grizelda Grimthorpe gathered
it up briskly and stuffed it back into the
clay bin, fastening the lid down firmly.

"Time I was off home," she said, putting on her coat and hat. A final glance around, a satisfied nod, and she picked up her broom and was gone.

Jeremiah watched from the darkened classroom as her plump figure on the old broom sailed across the high school gates and over the trees on the horizon. The silvery face of the moon shone down on the big white rat as it turned away from the window and pattered across the empty classroom. For a moment the rat paused by the clay bin, patted it gently and sighed. What a Friday this had been – the strangest Friday ever, perhaps.

Chapter 6

When Monday morning arrived, Miss Addle could scarcely believe her eyes! The Academy looked like a different school altogether. The teachers and children were all astonished by the change. In the new, improved, *ordered* Academy everyone worked harder.

From then on, every day, just as the

children were leaving, Grizelda arrived to clean up that day's spilled paint, and to sweep and dust every corner. Jeremiah was equally particular about eating up every dropped crumb or apple core! Ben and Sarah would wait at the front steps for Grizelda's arrival, to show her their latest art work or a new game they'd just learnt. Soon Grizelda would be surrounded by laughing pupils, all talking at once and clamouring for her attention.

That summer, Miss Addle entered the
school in the annual county art exhibition
for schools. To everyone's surprise –
everyone except one old, green-eyed lady
and one white rat, that is – the entries
from Miss Addle's Academy for Artistic
Children took First Prize in all categories,
with a Special Distinction being awarded
by the judges for the clay sculptures.

"Inspired effort . . . almost magical . . . enchanting vision. . ." were just some of the comments. "The clay almost seems to have a life of its own. . ." said one judge, who came closer than he could ever have known to the truth.

Miss Addle was delighted to receive a visit of congratulations from old Sir James Milligrew, the Chairman of the Academy Board of Trustees. He waved an important-looking envelope in the air.

60

"Good news, Miss Addle! Good news!" he cried. "The Board of Trustees asked the local authority for some help in funding the Academy, and your pupils have just done so well in the county art competition that they have agreed! Our money worries are over!"

"Pity about young Blockett," he said as he was leaving. "Between you and me, Miss Addle, he went a bit peculiar – had to go away for a long rest, you know. Wrote the most extraordinary report on the school – sheer gibberish about talking rats, and old ladies flying about with yellow buckets. Saw little purple men, you know – overwork, poor fellow!"

Miss Addle stood at the foot of the front steps, watching Sir James' shiny black car drive away. A short, stout figure on a rattly old bicycle pedalled slowly up the drive.

Really, thought Miss Addle, if I didn't know better, I'd swear Mrs Grimthorpe was a witch!

The End

Why do witches
ride broomsticks?

Because vacuum
cleaner cords aren't
long enough.

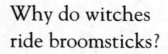

Why is the letter
T ticklish?

It makes a witch
twitch.

What do witches enjoy most
about school?

Spelling.

Broomstick
Services

Ann Jungman

Illustrated by Jan Lewis

For Margaret Barbalet
with love

Chapter 1

In the Car Park

On the outskirts of the town stood a brand new supermarket, surrounded by a huge concrete car park. During the day the car park bustled with busy shoppers but at night it was completely empty. Well, that was usually the case, but one dark November night anyone passing would have been surprised to see the most amazing sight.

In a little cluster of trees on one side of the car park were three witches, dancing round a cauldron. As they kicked their legs up in the air they sang at the tops of their voices:

"Bubble, bubble, toil and trouble,
Fire burn and cauldron bubble."

On a branch of one of the trees sat a black cat, howling in tune with the witches and waving his tail happily. After a while they stopped singing and dancing and sat round the fire.

"Let's think of something really wicked to do tonight," said the tallest witch, smiling in the moonlight.

"Something really horrible to punish those people who dared to build a car park on our sacred site."

"It's not that bad, Maud," said the smallest of the witches. "They weren't to know that this was our sacred site, and at least our special tree is still here."

"Not that bad?" spat out the tall witch. "Honestly, Ethel, I despair of you, I really do. Things are getting worse and worse for us witches. The twentieth century has been a disaster. When we were young we were always bumping into

other witches on their broomsticks. Now you never see anyone. I haven't had a broomstick crash for years. Soon it will be impossible to make any spells at all. And all you can do is make excuses for people. Now come on, both of you, help me think up a terrible and suitable revenge."

"We could make all the lights go out," suggested the third witch, a plump and jolly figure.

"Yes!" agreed Ethel. "They wouldn't like that one bit. And make all the televisions go off."

"And the heating," continued the plump witch, "and the electric blankets and the washing-machines and the videos and the computers and all the funny gadgets that people have in their houses these days."

"You're hopeless, absolutely hopeless, the pair of you," fumed the tall witch. "Thank goodness poor dear Mother isn't here to listen to the pathetic suggestions you're making. Now stop messing around and help me think of something really bad, really mean and horrible."

"Oh, Maud," sighed the plump witch, "you're such a dreamer. Why can't you just accept that witches have had it? We just don't fit any more – in this world full of supermarkets and televisions and cars and walkmans. We're as old-fashioned as

corsets and lavender and cucumber sandwiches, and I for one have had enough."

"Enough?" thundered Maud. "You miserable bat-faced apology for a witch! What do you mean you've had enough? Mabel, I demand an explanation."

"I've had enough of being a witch in the last part of the twentieth century and so I've decided to give it up. I'm going to be ordinary."

"Ordinary?" shrieked Maud. "What is that supposed to mean, you great soggy bag of mashed potatoes?"

Mabel flushed but looked hard into Maud's flashing eyes.

"What I mean, Maud, is that I'm going off into the world and I'm going to try and find a job and live like an ordinary person. I don't want to spend my time dancing round an old pot and riding around on an old broomstick, thinking up silly spells. I know when I'm beaten. No more witchery for me."

"Good!" shouted Maud. "You go then, and try and become an ordinary person. You'll soon find out what it's like out there. They won't want to know you. You'll be cold and lonely and hungry, but don't think Ethel and I will hang around waiting for you to come to your senses. We'll be off to some distant place and you may not be able to find us. Isn't that right, Ethel?"

"Well, actually, Maud," whispered Ethel, biting her nails and looking at the ground, "I think I'd like to go with Mabel. I'm tired of being a witch too."

"Worms, traitors, miserable toads!" thundered Maud. "Well, off you both go then, but I'm keeping the cauldron and the book of spells. I may be the last wicked witch left in the world, but I shall never desert the old ways of our mother and grandmother and the generations before them. I shall continue with our great ways till the end of time."

"Each to her own taste, Maud," said Mabel cheerfully. "We're very happy for you to keep the cauldron and the book of spells. Ethel and I will have no need of such things where we are going. Now, Maud dear, take good care of yourself and don't forget to wear your warmest knickers when the weather gets worse. You could catch your death of cold flying around up there. I do hope that when Ethel and I are settled you will come and visit us. We don't want to lose touch. I mean, we are still sisters, even if we have chosen different paths."

"Don't be ridiculous," yelled Maud. "I wouldn't lower myself by talking to creeps like you. Don't think you'll get away with this, because you won't. You'll come crawling back to me begging for forgiveness and, who knows, maybe I'll be in a good mood and help, or then again maybe I won't."

"Oh, dear," sighed Mabel. "I had hoped we'd manage an agreeable parting of the ways. Still, if you won't have it you won't. Well, our door will always be open to you, Maud, and I wish you well."

"Me, too," whispered Ethel. "And do please come to see us, Maud. I'd be so sad never to see you again."

With a last glance at Maud, Ethel and Mabel walked off hand in hand, down the road that led to the town. Mabel heard a little squeak as she strode off and when she looked down she saw their black cat running along beside them.

"Look, Ethel," she said happily, "Black Cat has decided to come with us."

As they walked away carrying their broomsticks, they could hear Maud behind them singing loudly:

"By toad in ditch and owl in tree,
Curses on those who abandon me."

"Can you hear that, Mabel?" whispered Ethel.

"Of course I can. She is fierce, isn't she? Still, courage, Ethel, courage. We had to do it and I expect Maud will come round eventually."

"I expect you're right, Mabel. I'm so tired I can't even think straight."

"What we need is some sleep," agreed Mabel. "Tomorrow we can plan our new life, when we feel fresh and it's daylight. Let's find somewhere to sleep."

"There's a hut over there."

"I can't read what it says on the board outside. We'll have to make some light. Come on, Ethel, there's no one around. Let's see if we can make the light spell work. Black Cat, you help too."

So the two witches raised their hands to the sky and chanted:

"By raven's toe and magpie's hoard,
Let light shine on yonder board."

Black Cat howled into the darkness in support.

A flash of lightning came out of nowhere and lit up the board.

"It worked," said Ethel proudly, cheering up a little.

"Yes," agreed Mabel, "and it says 'St Margaret's Primary School'. Well, that's good. Schools are empty at night. Come on, Ethel, we'll sleep in that hut and by the time the children come to school, we'll be well away."

"Are you sure it's safe, Mabel?"

"Don't be so wet, Ethel. Of course it's safe. Now come on, on to your broomstick and we'll just hop over the railings. One, two, three. Jump on, Black Cat, and over we go."

And within five minutes both the witches were fast asleep in the hut where the school caretaker kept his tools.

Chapter 2

In the Playground

The next day the children came to school as usual and played until the bell went for lessons to begin. The witches slept through it all. Playtime came and still the two witches slept. However, Black Cat, feeling bored and hungry, squeezed through a hole in the wall and began to walk round the playground. A group of children stopped playing ball and ran over to the cat.

"Look, a cat. Puss, puss, come here, puss, puss, puss," said Lucy, kneeling down to stroke him.

Black Cat didn't like children and he raced back to the hut as fast as he could. The three children followed.

"It's gone into the caretaker's hut," yelled Joe.

"We must have scared it," said Jackie. "Let's go and see if it wants some milk."

The children pulled the door of the hut open and there, snoring away, surrounded by spades and rakes and buckets, lay Mabel and Ethel. The sudden light and draught woke the two witches, who sat up and looked round at

their unusual surroundings, blinking and rubbing their eyes. The children looked at the witches and the witches looked at the children. The children couldn't believe their eyes.

"Well, come in," said Mabel eventually. "It's cold with the door open."

The children stepped inside and Joe shut the door behind them.

"You look like witches," he said in amazement.

"We are witches," Mabel told him. "But we're not the bad kind, well, not any more we're not."

"I'm not scared," said Lucy. "They're not witches. They're just trying to scare us. Let's go and tell the head."

Mabel leapt up and, holding her hands out, shouted:

"Little children! In a trice
You will all be furry mice."

"No, Mabel," cried Ethel, looking at the three mice running around on the floor of the shed, "not mice. Remember we've got Black Cat with us."

Black Cat was crouching and arching his back, preparing to leap on the mice.

"Little cat with coat so black,
From now on you will be a – a – coat
    rack."

A second later,
there in the tumble-
down hut, stood a lovely,
shiny wooden coat rack.

"Now you turn those
children back into
themselves," said Ethel
in an angry voice.
"Honestly, Mabel, that
was more like Maud
than you. Remember
we're supposed to be
changing our ways."

"Sorry, Ethel," said Mabel, sitting
down. "I just didn't think. They gave
me a shock and I did the first thing that
came into my head. Right, what is the
spell to turn mice into children? Oh
dear, Ethel, I've forgotten it."

Ethel shut her eyes and thought. Then she cried:

"*Little mice, one, two, three,*
Once again children be."

But the children went on being mice.
"It didn't work! Oh, Mabel, think hard."
Mabel burst out:

"*You three funny mice*
Be children sweet and nice."

But still nothing happened. "Oh, no, they're still mice. Try again, Ethel."

"Don't worry. I'm sure I've got it this time," said Ethel.

"You three furry, squeaky mice,
Be once more children in a trice."

Suddenly Joe, Lucy and Jackie stood in front of them again.

"I'm very sorry," began Mabel to the children. "I just wasn't thinking."

"No, we were asleep, you see," added Ethel. "You had better report us now, we've asked for it."

"You *are* witches!" burst out Jackie. "You really, really are!"

"That's right," said Mabel. "Now, come on, let's get it over with. Take us to the head, or whoever you think is the right person."

"You can't be bad witches," said Lucy. "If you had been you'd have let that cat eat us and escaped."

"What are you doing here, anyway?" demanded Jackie.

So Mabel explained about the quarrel with Maud and how she and Ethel had had enough.

"So, you see," said Mabel, "we want to be ordinary and the first thing we need to do is find a way to earn a bit of money, so that we can buy food. Can you help us?"

"Why should they help us, Mabel?" demanded Ethel. "If you'd turned me into a mouse with a cat nearby, I wouldn't want to help you."

"I'd like to help," said Joe. "This is the most exciting thing that's happened to me for ages."

"Yes," agreed Jackie. "Once the cat had been turned into a coat rack I enjoyed being a mouse."

Just then the bell for the end of playtime went but the children didn't want to go back to their classrooms.

"We must go," Jackie pointed out, "or

everyone will come looking for us and they'll find Mabel and Ethel. You two stay here. We'll bring you some food at lunchtime, and after school we'll have another talk and try to think of a way out of your problem."

Chapter 3

The Great Idea

As soon as school was over the children put their money together and bought some crisps and juice for the witches and some milk for Black Cat (for when he stopped being a coat rack) and raced over to the hut. While they sat round munching, they tried to think what the witches could do to earn money.

"You could sweep the streets with your broomsticks," suggested Joe.

"That won't do," replied Jackie. "They clean the streets with machines these days."

"You could sweep the leaves in the park in autumn," suggested Lucy.

"Yes," sniffed Mabel, "but what would we do the rest of the year?"

Jackie suddenly jumped up.

"I have a brilliant idea," she cried.

"All right, genius, let's hear it," said Joe.

"The broomsticks, do they work?" asked Jackie.

"Of course they do," said Ethel indignantly. "I mean we are witches after all, even if we do want to be like ordinary people."

"Good," said Jackie. "Then you could deliver to people living high up in tower blocks."

"What are you on about, genius?" asked Lucy.

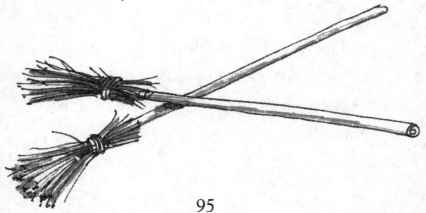

"You know what it's like in those high tower blocks. The lifts are always broken. People like my gran like to have fish and chips and things, but they don't want to walk down fifteen flights of stairs and then up again. Ethel and Mabel could deliver food through the windows."

"It's a great idea," said Joe. "Congratulations, Jackie, I'd never have thought of it."

"Yeah," agreed Lucy, "it's something that only someone who could ride a broomstick could do. It could be a real service."

"There is a problem," Joe pointed out. "Most people don't believe in witches and they won't take the idea seriously."

"That's true," agreed Mabel sadly, "and there are some who don't like us. They'd call the police in no time."

"I know what we have to do," cried Jackie. "We have to talk to my gran."

"What's your gran got to do with it?" asked Joe.

"She's the Chairperson of the Senior Citizens' Association and the Tenants' Association. That means she knows everyone who lives in the flats. If we could get her on our side, she could persuade all the others to give Ethel and Mabel a fair chance."

"I like your gran," said Joe. "She listens to us. Let's all go round and see if we can get her to agree to help."

"Yes, let's," agreed Lucy. "But, Ethel and Mabel, you must leave your hats and broomsticks here. Hang them on the coat rack. We don't want to give Jackie's gran a shock. We want her to get used to the idea slowly."

Reluctantly the witches agreed. They left their hats and brooms behind and followed the children to the block of flats. As the lift was broken they had to walk up fifteen flights.

"I can see why they'd want us to deliver to them," panted Mabel. "These stairs are terrible."

When they finally got to Jackie's gran's flat, they all trooped in.

"Hello, Jackie love. Hello, Joe and Lucy," said Gran. "Nice to see you. And who are these two ladies? I don't think I've ever met you before."

"No, you haven't. I'm Mabel and this is my sister, Ethel."

"Well, sit down. I'll make us a nice cup of tea. You all look very tired."

While they sat drinking their tea Ethel and Mabel looked round curiously.

"So this is how people live," said Ethel. "Very nice."

"What an odd thing to say," said Gran,

looking puzzled. "Whatever do you mean?"

"It's what we came to see you about, Gran," burst out Jackie. "You see we need your help very, very much."

"My help! Whatever for?"

"It's for Mabel and Ethel. You see they're both witches but they want to find work and earn a living, and we want to help them. Now, I've had this brilliant idea that they should deliver food and things on their broomsticks to people in the flats. I thought that if you agreed to explain to all the people who live in the flats, it might work."

"Just a minute. Are you trying to tell me these two ladies are witches?"

"Yes, we are witches," Mabel told her, "or at least we *were*."

"Don't be silly," said Gran. "Everyone knows witches don't exist. Is this some kind of a joke?"

"No, honestly," said Ethel. "We are witches, but good ones and we want to use our special abilities, like riding broomsticks, to help people and earn a living."

Gran burst out laughing.

"You're all playing a joke on me. Well, I like a good laugh. Pity it's not true. Having people to deliver food and shopping and laundry and things through the window would be wonderful. Nice idea."

"But it could come true," Ethel told her. "Honestly. Now listen, if we fly up to your window with your supper all hot and ready to eat, would you believe us?"

"I'd have to," laughed Gran.

"Right, let's have your order and off we go."

"I don't believe you can do it, but all right. I'll have a pizza. Here's some money. Buy three large ones. Jackie's Uncle Fred will be here soon and we can all share them for tea."

They all rushed back to the school and rescued the broomsticks and hats, and Ethel turned the coat rack back into Black Cat so that he could have his milk. Then they walked quickly to Pizza Hut and the children bought three different pizzas and handed them to Ethel and Mabel. The two witches flew as fast as they could to the block of flats.

Gran stood at her window, looking out with interest. At that moment Uncle Fred arrived. Gran quickly explained what was happening and Uncle Fred joined her at the window. When they saw the two witches on their broomsticks flying towards them, they couldn't believe their eyes.

"Three piping hot pizzas for number 273," said Mabel.

Eventually Gran found her voice.

"And they are piping hot too. Well, you'd better come in and we'll have a talk while we eat."

"We'll just fetch the children and then we'll be with you in two ticks."

To Uncle Fred's amazement, the children were soon sitting on the broomsticks and flying through the air with shrieks of excitement. He had to pinch himself to make sure he wasn't dreaming as Ethel, Mabel and the children flew through the window. Gran introduced the witches to Uncle Fred, and a few minutes later they were sitting round, drinking tea and eating slices of pizza. Everyone agreed that it looked as though Broomstick Services would go down very well.

"I think we should get it off to a flying start," said Joe.

Everyone groaned at the pun.

"No, seriously," he said. "We should have a grand opening night. Send out notices to everyone in the flats and then put on a big show, you know, music and lights, get it in the local paper, and everything. That way everyone in the area would get to know about Mabel and Ethel and they'd be busy every night."

"It's a smashing idea," said Mabel. "You are clever children. We were jolly lucky to meet you. We'd never have thought of all this on our own."

"Let's design a card now," said Gran.

"Let's see, what should it say? How about:

Is your lift always broken? Do you hate walking up hundreds of stairs? Is the shopping too heavy? Is the take-away always cold when you get it home? Now your problems are solved. Broomstick Services will bring you fast food or shopping to your very window. Fast, clean, efficient, reliable and cheap service. First orders taken on Friday night at 7 p.m. Don't miss this rare opportunity. BE AT YOUR WINDOWS. Free delivery on Friday night only."

"Sounds great," said Lucy. "Now we'll all have to work very hard writing these out. Then we'll have to deliver them before Friday."

"Ethel and I could do the cards," said Mabel. "If we had somewhere to stay we could do them all day and decorate them with hats and broomsticks and things."

"You can stay here," Gran offered. "It'll be a bit cramped but I like company. You're very welcome."

"Thanks," said Mabel. "We'd love to."

"Maud was so wrong," muttered Ethel. "She said no one would want us but so far everyone has been so kind. I'd have given up being a witch years ago if I'd known."

Chapter 4

The Opening Night

Gran called meetings of the Senior
Citizens' and the Tenants' Associations
and told them all about the wonderful
service that Mabel and Ethel were
offering. Some people had doubts about
allowing witches on to the estate but
Gran assured them that Ethel and Mabel

had definitely decided to give up doing wicked things and that their special skills would only be used to help people. Eventually it was agreed to give the witches one chance on the following Friday.

When Friday night came, everything was ready. Joe had borrowed as many tape recorders as he could and had recorded the rousing music of *The William Tell Overture* to accompany the opening flight. Lucy had gone round the flats and persuaded everyone to put their lights on at seven o'clock.

As seven o'clock approached, most of the people who lived in the flats were leaning out of their windows waiting to see what would happen. Mabel and Ethel brushed their long black locks

and put on their tall, shiny black hats.

"Five minutes to go," said Jackie. "Are you nervous?"

"Not me," said Mabel. "I'm looking forward to it. Fame at last."

Suddenly they heard a scream from Ethel.

"Ethel," said Mabel sternly, "pull yourself together. I won't tolerate a show of nerves at this stage, just when everyone has been so helpful."

"Our broomsticks," Ethel burst out. "Look, they've gone."

"Oh, no," groaned Mabel.

"What are we going to do?" demanded Joe. "Everyone is waiting."

"Maud, it must be Maud," exclaimed Mabel. "I wondered when she'd strike. Of all the low-down tricks."

Above them they heard a loud cackle. They looked up and there was Maud, her hair flowing in the wind, hovering on her broomstick overhead and clutching their broomsticks.

"What did you expect, dear sisters? I'm still a wicked witch. Did you expect fair play? You're even softer than I thought. Well, try and launch your little scheme now. See how much your new friends will like you when you let them down."

"Maud, you come here this minute and bring our broomsticks back."

"Never," yelled Maud defiantly. "I won't let you use witch magic to help people.

By toad in ditch and owl in tree,
Curses on those who challenge me."

And she flew off into the darkness, laughing loudly.

"Do something," yelled Joe. "There are only a couple of minutes to go. Everyone is waiting."

"Couldn't you magic some ordinary brooms or something?" said Lucy. "I mean, you're witches. Do they have to be the special twiggy kind of broomsticks?"

"I don't know," said Mabel. "I mean, it's never come up before. Get me a couple of brooms and we'll have a go."

The children rushed off.

"I knew something would happen to spoil it all," moaned Ethel.

"Be quiet," said Mabel firmly, "and start thinking about spells to magic brooms. All is not yet lost. We can

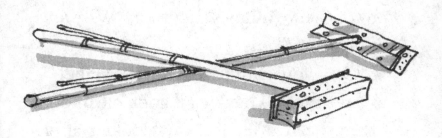

still show Maud a thing or two."

A few moments later the children returned clutching two squeegy mops.

"What on earth are those?" demanded Mabel.

"Squeegy mops. They're for cleaning floors too. They were the nearest thing we could find in a hurry. Will they do?"

"We'll have to give it a try," sighed Mabel.

"Well, hurry up. It's after seven o'clock and people are getting impatient."

All over the flats people were leaning

out of their windows shouting, "Why are we waiting?"

"Can you think of a spell, Mabel?" asked Ethel. "They've all gone clean out of my head. Maud always looked after the broomsticks and she's got the Magic Book."

"I'm going to try. Now quiet, everyone. Here we go:

Squeegy mop so bright and clean,
Hover now in the moon's beam.
Fly up, fly up, fly up so high,
Into the cold winter night sky."

They all looked hopefully at the squeegy mops. But nothing happened.

The cries of "Why are we waiting?" got louder.

Then Ethel burst out:

"I remember! I remember now! It only works if we do it standing on our heads. Come on, Mabel, not a moment to lose. One, two, three and upside down."

From the upside-down position the two witches repeated the spell. The children watched with bated breath. The two mops began to fly up into the air.

"Wait for us," yelled the two witches as they quickly stood up.

"They've got away," cried Jackie. "Get them back. You've got to get them back."

"*By witch's nose and giant's knee, I order you mops to return to me*," cried Ethel desperately.

The two mops came crashing down, sending the little group flying and knocking Mabel over.

"Well done, Ethel," said the children. "Now quick, we'll start the music and you can begin the real business of the evening."

"Come on, Mabel," Ethel told her sister. "No point in lying there in the mud. We've got work to do."

"Right," agreed Mabel, staggering to her feet and grabbing the mop firmly. "Come on, Black Cat, up you get behind."

But Black Cat hunched his back and hissed and, waving his tail, walked away.

"He won't come," said Mabel sadly. "He must think it would be undignified."

"Don't worry," said Lucy. "You don't really need him to fly with you, not tonight."

"Music starting on the count of three," shouted Joe. "One, two, three."

As the music blared out, the two witches rose in the air on the mops. A great cheer went up, as they flew round waving their hats in the air and blowing kisses. Then Ethel began taking orders and Mabel flew off to the various shops and restaurants to collect the food.

"Chicken for Mrs Barzetti," called Ethel. "Two kingsize hamburgers for the Brown twins, and sweet and sour pork for Mr Griffin at number 49."

All evening the witches flew around delivering piping hot food, chatting merrily to all their customers and finally taking away the empty cartons and putting them neatly in the dustbins.

When it was all over, everyone agreed that it had been a huge success and promised to use the witches' services on a regular basis and recommend them to their friends. That night Mabel and Ethel collapsed in Gran's flat, exhausted but happy.

"We did it, Ethel. We made it. We've got a job."

"I know," agreed her sister, "and we're making friends too. Maud couldn't have been more wrong."

"Poor old Maud," mused Mabel. "I wonder how long she'll keep it up. With a bit of luck she'll see how well we're doing and join us. It would be nice for the three of us to be together again, and Black Cat too. I wonder where he went."

"We'll just have to hope he turns up," said Ethel. "Now go to sleep. Tomorrow is going to be another hardworking day for Broomstick Services."

LAUNDRY

Chapter 5

Maud Joins In

Ethel and Mabel were a huge success. Every day they made flights to do people's shopping, to take washing to the laundrette, to collect medicines from the chemist and even to entertain children when they were bored. After a few weeks they were offered a flat on the thirty-fifth floor, which no one wanted because it was too high up. The two witches were thrilled to bits and busily set about painting it. When that was done, they went out and bought some pieces of secondhand furniture and a television.

"Fancy us having a place of our own, Mabel," said Ethel happily. "I wonder what Maud would say if she could see us now."

"I hope she's all right," answered Mabel. "It's a cold winter. I wish we could have sent her a change-of-address card but we don't know where to find her."

"She found us when she wanted to be mean to us," Ethel pointed out. "She'll find us if she needs us. Would you like

another cup of tea, Mabel dear? There's a good film on the television starting in a few minutes."

So the witches sat drinking tea and watching television and enjoying the warmth and cosiness of their own home. They were just about to turn the television off, when they heard a knock on the window.

"Must be the wind," said Mabel.

"Must be," agreed Ethel.

But the knocking went on. The sisters looked at each other. Then they heard a cat miaowing.

"It is! It must be! It's Maud and Black Cat," cried Ethel, pulling back the curtain, and there, hovering on her broomstick, was their sister.

"Come on in," cried Mabel, opening the window. Maud flew in, wet and shivering.

"You need a hot bath," declared Ethel. "Come on, Maud, come and see our lovely bathroom."

Rather to Mabel's surprise, Maud allowed herself to be led to the bathroom and put into a steaming bubble bath. Mabel quickly heated up some soup and when Maud emerged, she was seated in front of the fire and given the soup. Black Cat, who was skinny, wet and miserable, was given food too.

"How did you find us?" asked Ethel.

"I've been trying to find you for ages. It was lonely without you. Being wicked was no fun on my own. So I said to Black Cat here, let's go and find them, and we did."

"We've done very well since we left, as you can see. We've got good work, a lovely place to live and lots of friends. Now, what do you say to that?"

"All right, I was mistaken. There's no

need to rub it in. I thought that people wouldn't accept witches but I was wrong. I've come here to say that I'm sorry about that rotten trick I played on you and I've brought your broomsticks back to prove it. And I wonder, could I please stay with you two?"

"Is this a trick, Maud?" asked Ethel suspiciously.

"No!" cried Maud. "I'm cold and I'm hungry and I'm lonely. You can see that I am."

"Then you'd better come and live with us here and help us with our work," said Mabel, smiling broadly. "We could do with some extra help. You see, Maud, they want us to take on a new service, called 'Meals on Broomsticks'. We'll need an extra pair of hands and

another broomstick if we're going to cope."

"Whatever is that?" demanded Maud.

"It's a service to deliver hot meals to people who find it hard to cook for themselves. It's usually called 'Meals on Wheels'. The problem is that by the time the meals have been carried up twenty flights of stairs they're cold. If we deliver them on our broomsticks, they'll still be all lovely and hot."

"Good," said Maud. "All I need is a good night's sleep and I'll be ready to go."

"You will be nice to people, won't you?" asked Ethel, looking worried. "You must promise not to scare them away."

"Maybe I will and maybe I won't. I'll just have to see if being good suits me as well as it suits you. Until I make up my mind, you'll just have to trust me, sisters dear."

However, Maud did very well. She flew around all day fetching and delivering and being every bit as pleasant as the other two. In fact, she became even more helpful than Ethel and Mabel, working till midnight and getting up first thing in the morning.

Chapter 6

A Witch Wedding

After a while Maud even began cooking special dishes for ill people: rice pudding and apple purée, beef broth and healthy chicken soup.

Her sisters didn't mind Maud cooking so long as she would leave them to sit in front of the television eating some

delicious take-away food. But Maud insisted that they help her, fetching and carrying, stirring, measuring and chopping.

Mabel and Ethel got so fed up they went round to see Gran.

"It's terrible," they burst out. "She makes us work all the time. We can't watch the television or listen to music or chat to our friends or sleep in late on Sundays. There's always something she makes us do."

"Oh, dear," said Gran, laughing. "She certainly is being good."

"You can say that again," groaned Mabel. "*And* she makes us say our prayers before we get into bed, even when it's very, very cold. It's just like it used to be when we were bad witches, being bossed about by Maud all the time."

"She even made us go to church *four* times last Sunday," added Mabel. "We like going to church. We always go to church now, but four times is a bit much."

"Oh, dear," agreed Gran. "I don't know what to suggest."

"I do," said Jackie. "The genius strikes again."

"All right, let's hear it," said Mabel. "Your last idea was a winner."

"Uncle Fred said she was a very

handsome woman," announced Jackie.

"So what?" moaned the witches.

"Fred!" exclaimed Gran. "My son Fred? Don't be daft. He's terrified of women. He never looks at them."

"Well, he looked at her," insisted Jackie. "Maybe they could get married."

"An excellent idea," agreed Gran. "I've wanted to see Fred married for years. I'll invite you all to dinner, and Fred too. Jackie, you, Lucy, Joe and your mum and dad must join us – so that it isn't too obvious. Next Saturday all right?"

"Yes," said Mabel, "but fancy Maud getting married. I can't imagine it."

"Bet you couldn't imagine her giving up being a bad witch, or turning into such a hard worker or you living in a flat and having friends. Isn't that right?"

"Yes," said Mabel, "but this is different. I mean, Maud was the wickedest witch I knew. And as for one of us getting married, well, I never even thought of it."

"It's worth a try," announced Ethel. "We've got nothing to lose and she's driving us round the bend at the moment."

"Umm," said Mabel, "I have an idea. How about a little love potion in their drinks? I think I remember enough spells to be able to do that. Let's have a think. Ah yes, I think I remember:

Little potion in a tick,
Make the drinker lovesick.
They will sigh and moan and weep,
Until they find true love to keep."

"That's it!" cried Ethel. "Oh, Maud, you don't know what we're cooking up for you. Hee, hee! What fun!"

So the next Saturday they all arrived at Gran's flat. Maud was looking rather miserable because Ethel had put some of the potion in her tea in the morning and Mabel had put some in her coffee after lunch. There stood Maud, Ethel, Mabel, Jackie, Jackie's mum and dad and Lucy and Joe, with flowers and a bottle of wine and a box of chocolates, waiting for the door to be opened.

"Come on in," said Gran. "Oh, what

lovely things! Are they for me? You are kind. Maud, you're looking lovely. I think you know everyone except my son, Fred."

Fred did not look very cheerful either. Ethel had been flying into his flat whenever he was out and putting the love potion on his toothbrush. But he cheered up very quickly when he saw Maud and soon they were chatting away happily together.

By the end of the evening he was going to show her round the local museum and she had invited him to supper the following week.

To cut a long story short, the love

potion worked very well and within two months the happy couple were engaged to be married.

"The only thing that worries me," Maud told her sisters, "is leaving you two in the lurch. I mean, it was kind of you to take me in after the trick I played on you. I feel bad about leaving you on your own."

"Don't give it a thought," Mabel assured her quickly. "Yes, we'll be sorry to lose you, Maud, of course we will, but we must think of your happiness. Just think how pleased dear Mother would have been. She was a married witch herself. She believed in marriage."

"Mother would have never forgiven us if we'd been selfish at a moment like this," added Ethel, biting her lip.

"You're right," agreed Maud. "We must do what Mother would have wished. I shall leave you the cauldron and the books. I am about to begin a new life. I shall go on working with you as before, of course, but other than that I shall forget all about witchcraft. Now, come on and help me choose a dress for the wedding."

Ethel whispered to Mabel, "Whew, that was a close thing! I thought for one terrible moment that she was going to stay with us."

"I know," agreed Mabel, "but we talked her out of it, thank goodness! After the wedding we'll be free again. Whoopee!"

When Jackie's mum and dad heard that Maud was going to marry Fred, they were very surprised.

"I'd completely given up on you, Fred," said Mum, giving him a big kiss.

"I'd given up on myself," laughed Fred, "but the first minute I saw Maud I knew she was the one."

"Congratulations, Fred," said Dad. "Great news."

So two weeks later Maud was married. It was much like any other wedding, except that the bride wore a long white dress with a witch's hat on her head and arrived on her broomstick with her two sisters.

After the ceremony there was a huge reception. All the people from the flats came and the local fast-food sellers all came too and gave the food for free. Everyone ate and ate and ate, pizzas and curry, Chinese food and kebabs, fish and chips and ice-cream. No one in the flats could remember when they had last had such a good time. When the time came for the happy couple to leave, Maud reached for her broomstick, and yelled:

"Jump up behind, Fred."

Away they flew out of the window with Black Cat perched behind them, while everyone waved and threw confetti.

"I never thought to see my Fred married," wept Gran. "Ethel and Mabel, you've made an old woman very happy."

"Thank Jackie," said Ethel, "not us. It was all her idea."

"Right," agreed Jackie. "I'm a genius or maybe I'm a witch."

"Worse things you could be," said her gran.

"Umm, I think that's what I'll be when I grow up," Jackie told her. "A witch."

Everyone thought it was an excellent idea and there was a toast to Maud, the married witch; to Ethel and Mabel, the good witches; and to Jackie, the witch-to-be.

Why did the witch
stay home from
school?

She had a *wicked* cold.

What do witches like for
breakfast?

Rice Crispies because
they snap-*cackle*-pop.

Knock knock
Who's there?
Witch.
Witch who?
Which one of you is going
to fix my broomstick?

Fisherwitch

SUSAN GATES

Illustrated by Rhian Nest James

For Phillip Rashidi

Chapter 1

It's the hot season in our part of
Africa. The lake near our village is
drying up. Sensible people stay indoors
or go out under umbrellas to keep off the
sun.

But my little brother Moses isn't
sensible. He keeps pestering me. "Come
out and play with me, Precious."

My mum is at the market. My dad is mending his fishing nets. So I've got to look after Moses.

"It's too hot to play," I tell him.

But Moses is already running outside into the sunshine.

Grandma's working at her sewing-
machine. She looks up and says, "Be
careful. It's very hot today. The kind of
day when Fisherwitch comes out the
lake. Fisherwitches are very sneaky
people so keep your eyes open. Keep

your ears open. And if you hear anything strange, see anything strange, don't hang around. Run straight back home to me!"

Moses and I laugh. We think it's just one of her stories. Gran has lots of stories about witches and spirits and zombies. If you believed all of them you'd be too scared to go out the door! And, besides, even if the story were true, how could Gran protect us against a witch? She's a tiny, skinny old gran. A puff of wind would blow her away.

"Okay, Gran, okay," we laugh. "We'll be careful!"

As soon as I step out the house I smell a revolting pong – a dreadful, fishy stink.

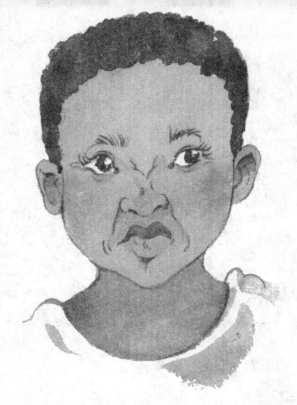

"Phew," says Moses, wrinkling up his nose. "What's that smell?"

I shrug. "I don't know. It's very strange. I've never smelled it before."

Then we hear a strange noise. It's coming from the reeds at the edge of our lake, near the weaver-bird tree.

But weaver-birds don't make noises like that.

Clack, clack, it goes. *Clack, clack.*

Moses is a very inquisitive boy. He wants to know everything that's going on.

"What's that noise?" he says. And he starts walking towards the reeds.

159

I'm beginning to get worried now. I'm his big sister and I'm responsible for him. And I can't help remembering Gran's warning: "If you hear anything strange, see anything strange. . ."

I've just seen something strange! Right down by my feet. I see ten long scratches

in the sand. I don't know an animal that leaves a trail like that. A hyena doesn't, a crocodile doesn't. And it leads right down to the reeds where the clacking noise is coming from.

"Come back, Moses," I yell at my brother. "There's something funny going on here. Something I don't like at all."

Moses stops. For once, I think to myself, he's going to do as he's told.

But then, from out of the reeds, comes
the strangest thing of all. It looks like a
ball. But it's floating above the ground
like a bright blue cloud. It glows like a
jewel. And a thousand tiny rainbows are
sparkling in it.

Chapter 2

As soon as Moses sees it he holds out his arms. "What a pretty thing!" he cries. "I want that pretty thing for myself!"

And he runs to catch it.

I feel a chill in my heart. I know that there's danger here somewhere.

"Don't go, Moses." I try to pull him back.

But Moses is very stubborn. When he wants something he never gives up. He rushes after the beautiful blue ball.

It floats away, just out of his reach.

Moses runs to grab it. He's almost touching it! But it darts away in a blue flash, quick as a kingfisher. It won't let him catch it. Every time he gets close it whisks away. He chases it.

And it's leading him closer and closer to the reeds by the lake.

"Moses," I shout. "Come back. This is some kind of trick. I'm sure it is!"

But Moses takes no notice. The shiny blue ball disappears into the reeds. And Moses runs after it.

There is silence for two seconds. Then Moses yells, "Precious, help me, Precious!"

I run into the reeds. They're taller than my head. I force them apart with my hands. I search high and low. But I can't find Moses or the blue ball.

They've both vanished. And all that's left is a fishy pong and ten snaky tracks. . .

I can't think what to do. I yell, "Moses, Moses!"

No answer.

I rush back home. But my mum isn't back, or my dad. Only Grandma's here and she's too old to help.

"Moses followed a blue ball!" I tell her. "He went after it into the reeds and I can't find him!"

Grandma looks up quickly from her sewing. She narrows her eyes.

"Did this ball dance in the air?" she asks. "And did it dart away when Moses got close?"

"Yes, yes."

"Then Fisherwitch is back!" says Gran. "She's back hunting for children. I told you to be careful! That ball Moses followed was a witchball. Fisherwitch uses them to catch children. When children chase them, they run right into her trap!"

"I smelled a fishy smell!" I tell Gran. "I heard something go *Clack, clack.* I saw ten snaky tracks!"

"That's Fisherwitch all right," says Gran. "Those are the tracks of her long sharp nails. Her nails that go *Clack, clack.* Quick, we must hurry. There's no time to lose. If we don't hurry, we'll never see Moses again!"

We rush outside. My heart's beating very fast. "Please let us be in time," I whisper to myself.

Grandma sniffs. She sniffs again. "I know that smell," she says. "That pong of rotting fish. I haven't smelled it for fifty years. But it's a smell you never forget. Fisherwitch is definitely back!"

Chapter 3

We creep along the lake shore.

"Shhhh!" says Grandma.

She parts some tall reeds.

I peep through. And see a fearful sight.

It's Fisherwitch. She's fast asleep. She's naked as a hippo, old and lumpy as a baobab tree. She's big as an elephant. Her skin is grey and baggy like an elephant's skin. Little red crabs are running in and out of its folds.

Phew, the pong is awful! You would need a whole shopful of perfume to make her sweet again!

She's got long yellow nails, as long as the canoes that fish on our lake. Her nails drag on the ground. They're very sharp, like spears.

She's made herself a shelter of fishbones to shade her from the sun.

"Where are you, Moses?" whispers
Gran. "Are you round here somewhere?"

Fisherwitch snores. Tiny shrimps
tumble out her hair.

My heart's beating so loud I'm scared
it will wake her.

Then we hear a very small voice. "Here I am. I'm trapped in her nails."

Fisherwitch has put her long nails together, like a cage. A big, frightened eye peeps out from inside. It's my brother Moses!

"I can't get out!" he says.

He pokes his fingers through the bars of his cage. I creep forward. I can hold his hand, but I can't get him out.

"What do we do now?" I beg Gran. I'm almost crying.

But Gran doesn't cry. She stays cool.

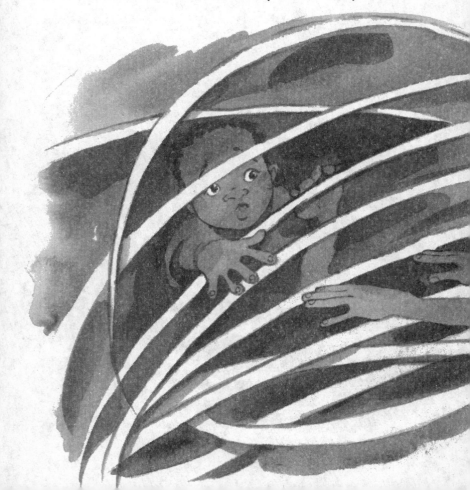

There's a fierce look in her eyes. A look I haven't seen before.

"Come with me," she hisses. She pulls me away.

"We can't leave Moses."

"We're coming straight back. But we must hurry. If Fisherwitch wakes up. . ."

I have to let go of Moses' fingers. "Don't leave me!" he says. But I have to run after Gran.

"What will she do with him?" I ask Gran. "What will she do with my brother?"

Gran's voice is grim. "She plans to eat him," she says.

"Oh, no!"

"Oh, yes. She will definitely eat him, unless we can save him. A Fisherwitch doesn't often catch children. Usually they catch fish. They stab them with their long, sharp nails. They thread fish on their nails like shish kebabs.

Sometimes they have twenty silver fish flapping on each of their nails! And they munch them, bones and all, when they feel like a snack. But when it gets very hot and the lake starts to dry up and there aren't many fish, then Fisherwitch gets hungry. Her belly begins to rumble. And she comes into the villages, hunting for children!"

"She won't shish kebab Moses, will she?"

"She will," says Gran, "unless we stop her. And if she doesn't shish kebab him straight away, she'll drag him into the lake. Like crocodiles do. She'll take him down to her dark cave. And keep him prisoner there until she feels like nibbling something."

"How do you know all this about Fisherwitches?" I ask Gran as we hurry back to our house.

"That's another story," says Gran. "No time for it now. Fisherwitch will soon wake up. Her belly will rumble. And then – no more Moses!"

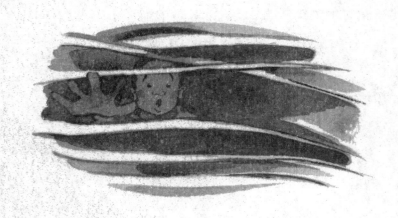

Chapter 4

I stumble after Gran. In my mind I can see my brother's poor frightened eyes, his tiny fingers reaching through the fingernail cage. But what can we do? We're helpless against the power of Fisherwitch.

But my little gran isn't helpless. She's fierce and determined. She rushes to her sewing-machine, picks up the heavy iron shears she uses to cut material.

"Quick, quick!" she says. "Fisherwitch is waking up!"

"How do you know?"

"Listen!"

I hear it too. A noise like a lion's roar:
GRRRRRRR! It makes the ground shake.
It's coming out of the reeds. It's
Fisherwitch's empty belly, rumbling.

We run back. We trample through the
reeds. Fisherwitch isn't awake yet. But
she's twitching in her sleep. She spits
out a fish-head.

There's no time to lose.

Gran raises her shears high. They glitter in the sun. She begins to hack through Fisherwitch's nails. It's very hard work – they're tough as elephants' toenails.

I hold my breath. One nail falls off! Moses pokes out his arm. "I'm nearly free!"

But Fisherwitch is waking up. Her eyelids flutter. One slides up. I see a cold, green eye swivel in our direction.

Grandma doesn't panic. She carries on cutting. Snap, snap. Another nail falls to the sand.

"I'm free!" says Moses. He wriggles out of his cage.

Fisherwitch yawns. With one long, yellow nail she scratches her itchy

places. Then she tries to scratch her back. But there's no nail to scratch with! My gran has just cut it off.

Fisherwitch is suddenly wide awake. She screams with rage. She stands up, in a shower of fish scales all green and gold.

"Who has cut my nails?" she howls.
"My beautiful long nails. And who has
stolen my dinner?"

Then she spots us, just as we're
creeping off through the reeds.

"You!" she hisses. "You cut my nails!"

She's hopping mad! Blue fire sizzles
from her eyes.

"Run, run," says Gran.

But Fisherwitch is right behind! She's howling, spitting fish-bones. She's got eight nails left and they're all sharp as spears.

We run towards our village, dragging Moses with us. But however fast we run, Fisherwitch is on our heels. *Thud, thud, thud!* For a big old witch she can run very fast!

"Help, help, save us!" But no one hears. They're all indoors, where it's nice and cool.

Fisherwitch is jabbing at us – trying to stab us like fish. Soon we'll be flapping on those long sharp nails!

But our house is right here. We tumble inside. Push a bed against the door, then sit down on it, gasping for breath.

Chapter 5

"We're safe now," I say. "She can't get us now!"

"I wouldn't be too sure," says Gran.

There's a scratching noise going up the walls.

"What's that?" says Moses, his eyes wide with fear.

Clack, clack, clack, clack, go Fisher-witch's nails.

"She's climbing on to the roof," says Grandma.

Sharp yellow claws come sliding
through our grass roof They jab about
trying to find us.

They stab a water melon and a sack of
maize.

"Ah ha, got you!" screams Fisher-witch.

Moses and I dive under the bed.

But Gran isn't scared. "I'll tell you, shall I," she says, "how I know so much about Fisherwitches?"

"Now is no time for stories!" I shout from under the bed.

Jab, jab, go Fisherwitch's nails. She stabs the mattress and hauls it up through the roof

"Get under the bed, Gran!" I beg.

But Gran will not hide. She stands strong as a termites' nest. And shouts out her story so Fisherwitch, squatting up on our roof, can hear her.

"Do you remember, Fisherwitch?" calls Gran. "Fifty years ago when you last came to this village? And you stole a

little girl called Rosebud? She had braids and blue beads in her hair? Well, that little girl was my best friend. And I've been waiting all this time, Fisherwitch, for you to pay another visit."

My tiny gran takes out her heavy iron shears. With eight swift blows she chops off every one of Fisherwitch's nails.

"Aieee!" screams Fisherwitch from the roof "You have killed me!"

Then there is silence. We wait a long time. Very cautiously, we open the door and peep out of the house.

There's nothing outside but a blue witchball. It's floating high above the ground.

"Don't you chase it this time," I warn Moses.

"I'm not that stupid!" he says.

The witchball hovers above us for a moment. It darts away, high into the sky. It goes higher, higher until it's just a blue dot. Then, with a bright orange flash, it burns up in the sun.

"Is she dead?" I ask Gran.

"Who knows?" says Gran. "Fisher-witches are very sneaky people. She might be dead. And she might not. She might hide out somewhere until her nails grow again."

I shiver. "I hope she's *really* dead."

"Well, if she isn't and she comes hunting children we know what to do."

My fierce little gran lifts up her iron shears. They glitter in the sun. *Snap, snap*, they go. *Snap, snap!*

The End

What do you say to
an angry witch?

Ribbit!

What is a witch's favorite part of a
newspaper?

The *Horror*-scopes!

Knock knock
Who's there?
Ron.
Ron who?

Ron faster, there's a witch after us!